Shoes from Grandpa

Mem Fox
illustrated by Patricia Mullins

SCHOLASTIC
SYDNEY AUCKLAND NEW YORK TORONTO LONDON

Late one summer Jessie's father invited all the family over for a barbecue.

When Grandpa saw Jessie he stood back and said,
'My, how you've grown!
You'll need a new pair of shoes this winter,
and I'll buy them.'

'Thanks a lot, Grandpa,' said Jessie.

And her dad said,
'I'll buy you some socks from the local shops,
to go with the shoes from Grandpa.'

And her mum said,
'I'll buy you a skirt that won't show the dirt,
to go with the socks from the local shops,
to go with the shoes from Grandpa.'

And her cousin said,
'I'll look for a blouse with ribbons and bows,
to go with the skirt that won't show the dirt,
to go with the socks from the local shops,
to go with the shoes from Grandpa.'

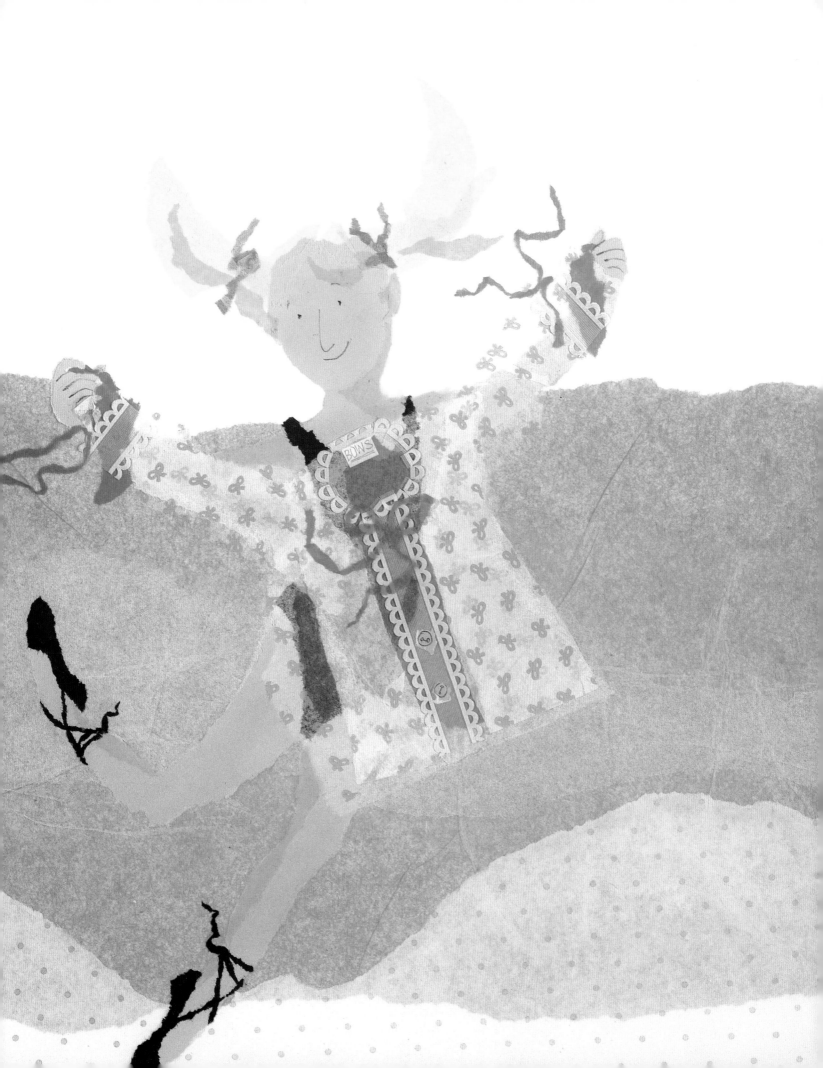

And her sister said,
'I'll get you a sweater when the weather gets wetter,
to go with the blouse with ribbons and bows,
to go with the skirt that won't show the dirt,
to go with the socks from the local shops,
to go with the shoes from Grandpa.'

And her grandma said,
'I'll find you a coat you could wear on a boat,
to go with the sweater when the weather gets wetter,
to go with the blouse with ribbons and bows,
to go with the skirt that won't show the dirt,
to go with the socks from the local shops,
to go with the shoes from Grandpa.'

And her auntie said,
'I'll knit you a scarf that'll make us all laugh,
to go with the coat you could wear on a boat,
to go with the sweater when the weather gets wetter,
to go with the blouse with ribbons and bows,

to go with the skirt that won't show the dirt,
to go with the socks from the local shops,
to go with the shoes from Grandpa.'

And her brother said,
'I'll find you a hat you can put on like that,
to go with the scarf that'll make us all laugh,
to go with the coat you could wear on a boat,
to go with the sweater when the weather gets wetter,
to go with the blouse with ribbons and bows,
to go with the skirt that won't show the dirt,
to go with the socks from the local shops,
to go with the shoes from Grandpa.'

And her uncle said,
'I'll buy you some mittens that are softer than kittens,
to go with the hat you can put on like that,
to go with the scarf that'll make us all laugh,
to go with the coat you could wear on a boat,

to go with the sweater when the weather gets wetter,
to go with the blouse with ribbons and bows,
to go with the skirt that won't show the dirt,
to go with the socks from the local shops,
to go with the shoes from Grandpa.'

And Jessie said,
'You're all so kind that I hate to be mean,
but please would one of you buy me some jeans?'

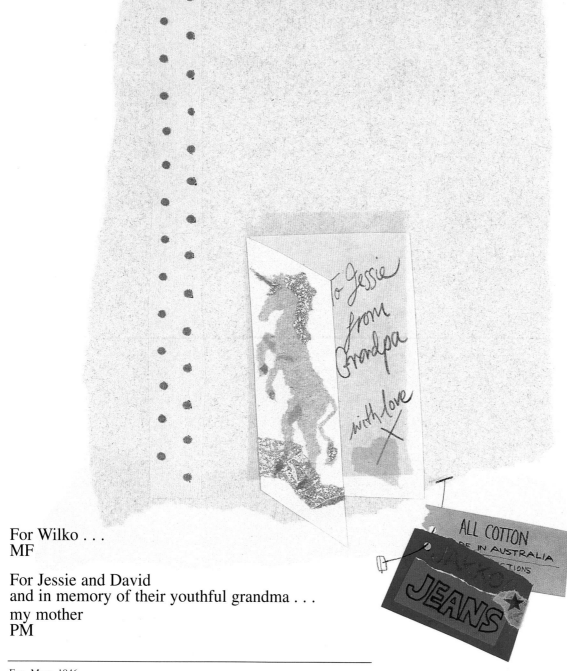

For Wilko . . .
MF

For Jessie and David
and in memory of their youthful grandma . . .
my mother
PM

Fox, Mem, 1946–.
    Shoes from grandpa.

    ISBN 0 86896 371 2.
    ISBN 978 0 86896 372 3 (pbk).

    1. Children's poetry, Australian. I. Mullins, Patricia 1952–. II. Title.

A821'3

Text copyright © Mem Fox, 1989.

Illustrations copyright © Patricia Mullins, 1989.

First published in 1989 by Scholastic Australia Pty Limited ACN 000 614 577,
PO Box 579, Gosford 2250. Also in Sydney, Brisbane, Melbourne, Adelaide and Perth.
www.scholastic.com.au

Reprinted in 1991(twice), 1993, 1994, 1995, 1996, 1998, 1999, 2001, 2003, 2004, 2005 (twice), 2006, 2007 (twice), 2008 and 2009 (twice).

Typeset by Excel Imaging, St. Leonards NSW.

Printed in Hong Kong.

25 24 23 22 21 20   9 / 0   0 1 2 3 4 5 / 1